A CLOSER LOOK

MARY McCARTHY

GREENWILLOW BOOKS
An Imprint of HarperCollins Publishers

Handmade papers and collage were used to prepare the full-color art.
The text type is 68-point Banjoman Text Bold.

Library of Congress Cataloging-in-Publication Data
McCarthy, Mary, (date).
A closer look / by Mary McCarthy.
  p. cm.
"Greenwillow Books."
Summary: Detailed collage illustrations accompanied by simple text present
expanding views of familiar objects in nature, such as a bug and a flower.
ISBN-13: 978-0-06-124073-7 (trade bdg.) ISBN-10: 0-06-124073-7 (trade bdg.)
ISBN-13: 978-0-06-124074-4 (lib. bdg.) ISBN-10: 0-06-124074-5 (lib. bdg.)
[1. Nature—Fiction.] I. Title.
PZ7.M+ [E] 22 2006029459

First Edition 10 9 8 7 6 5 4 3 2 1

Greenwillow Books

For my dad

Look!

What do you . . .

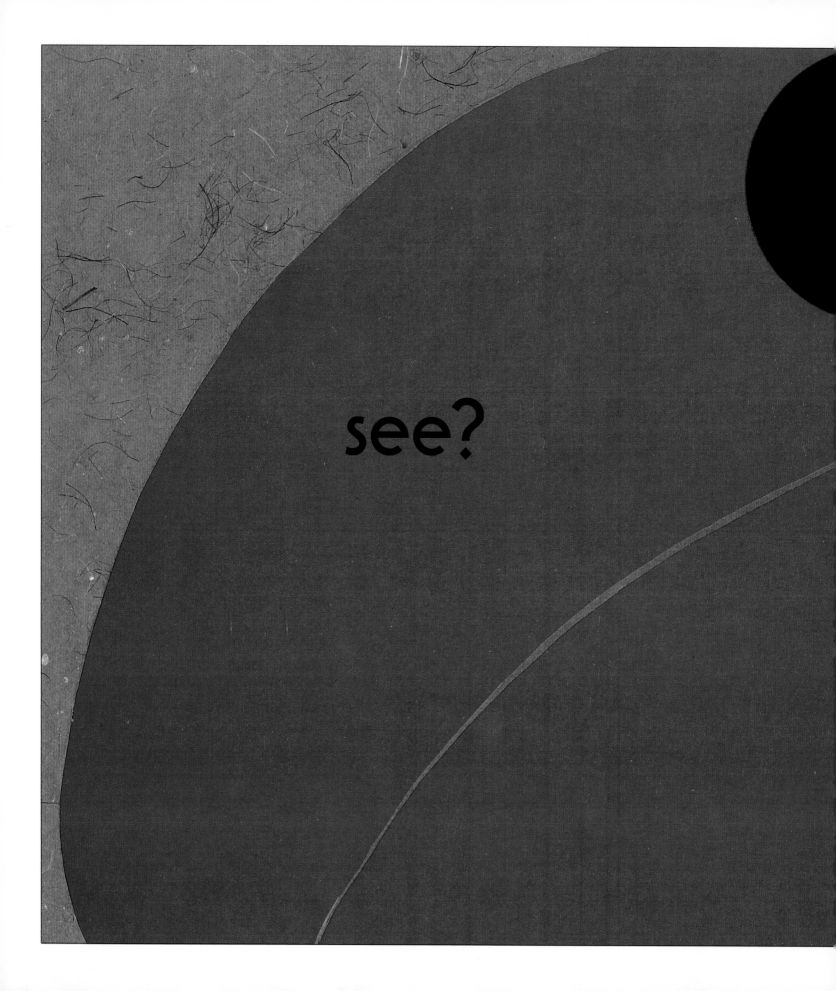

see?

A bug.

Look!

What do you . . .

see?

A flower.

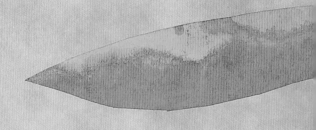

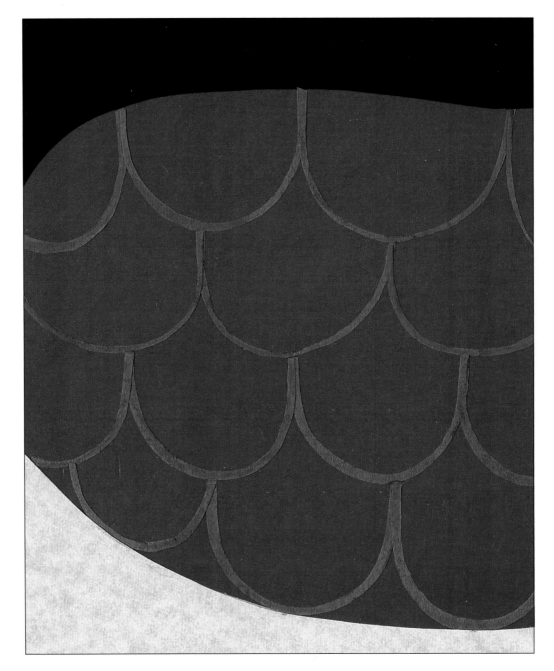

What do you . . .

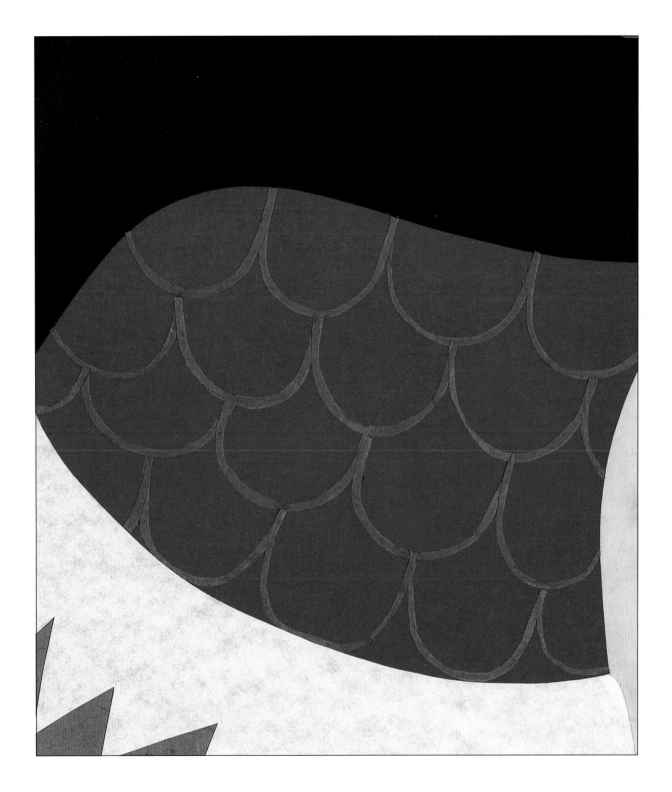

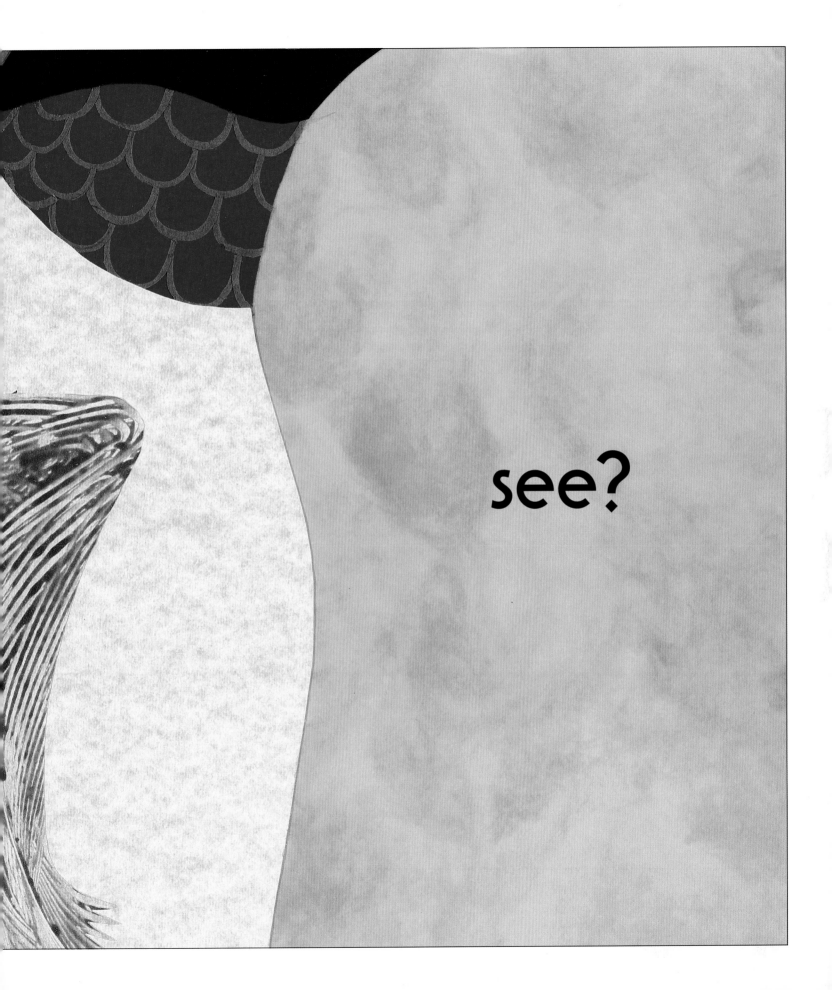

see?

A bird.

Look again.

What do
you see?

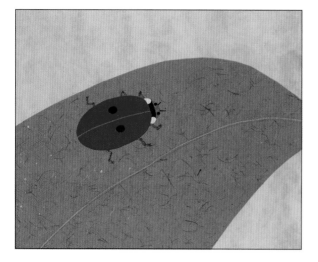

Ladybugs are a type of beetle. They are small and round, and are often red with black spots. They can have many spots or just two. Ladybugs with two spots sleep during the winter. Ladybugs are good for gardens. They eat tiny bugs that are bad for plants.

Cardinal flowers are found mostly in wet meadows, swamps, and along streams. They have bright red petals and bloom at the same time every year. Cardinal flowers are the favorite flower of some hummingbirds.

Hummingbirds use their long, slender beaks to drink the nectar inside flowers. They are small birds that can fly upside down, backward, and forward. The one in this book is called a ruby-throated hummingbird.